How the Nobble Was Finally Found

C. K. Williams
AND
Stephen Gammell

HARCOURT CHILDREN'S BOOKS

Houghton Mifflin Harcourt

BOSTON NEW YORK 2009

ONCE UPON A TIME there was something, a creature or an animal or a person or, anyway, a something named a Nobble, who—even though he'd lived about four thousand three hundred and twenty-three years and three months and fourteen days—had never been discovered, or bumped into, or met, or found by anybody, anybody at all.

He lived all alone.

The Nobble, who had huge eyes and dangly ears and long hair and two lovely wings and little claws on his fingers and a bunch of nice toes, sometimes thought he might be invisible, because he'd been hanging around for such a long time without anybody ever finding him. But it wasn't really that he was invisible; it's just that the places where the Nobble spent his time, nobody else ever went.

He used to take his naps, for instance, in the bottom rung of the number eight, and you don't come across too many other things in the number eight, or not often, anyway. And sometimes he went to play in the space between Wednesday and Thursday, and naturally you'd have to expect that he'd be mostly by himself there, because in that little space there really wasn't much to see at all, except way off in the distance a little glow like a radio dial that the Nobbie decided was probably something even farther away, between Friday and Saturday, maybe.

Now you'd have to expect that the Nobble would sometimes become a little lonely, being either invisible or always in a place where nobody ever went. He tried not to be sad, though; he'd just sigh—he was very patient after all this time—and sit awhile and curl his wings up over his dangly ears. And although sometimes a little tear or two would come out of his huge eyes, he'd just take another walk along the veins of the leaves of an elm tree, or on the bumps under the word asparagus, or maybe he'd swim in the river that runs along beneath piano strings, or put his nice toes out in front of him and just follow where they went.

But if you think that sometimes the Nobble might cry a little in his sleep, and pretty loudly, too, you'd be right, because even though he mostly liked being who he was, sometimes it was sad, never meeting anybody, anybody at all besides himself. Sometimes the Nobble would even think that not only was he dreaming that he was crying in his sleep, but maybe he was a dream himself; maybe he was just himself having a dream about himself.

And he'd think that maybe in another dream he'd be somebody who didn't live quite as much alone as he did—you know, in the little octagonal rooms in snowflakes, and in the big tangled places in the wind. And when he thought that, the NOBBLe would try to wake himself up by pinching himself. Once he even pinched himself so hard that he shouted out in his sleep, "Ouch!" and woke up, and had to put on a Band-Aid.

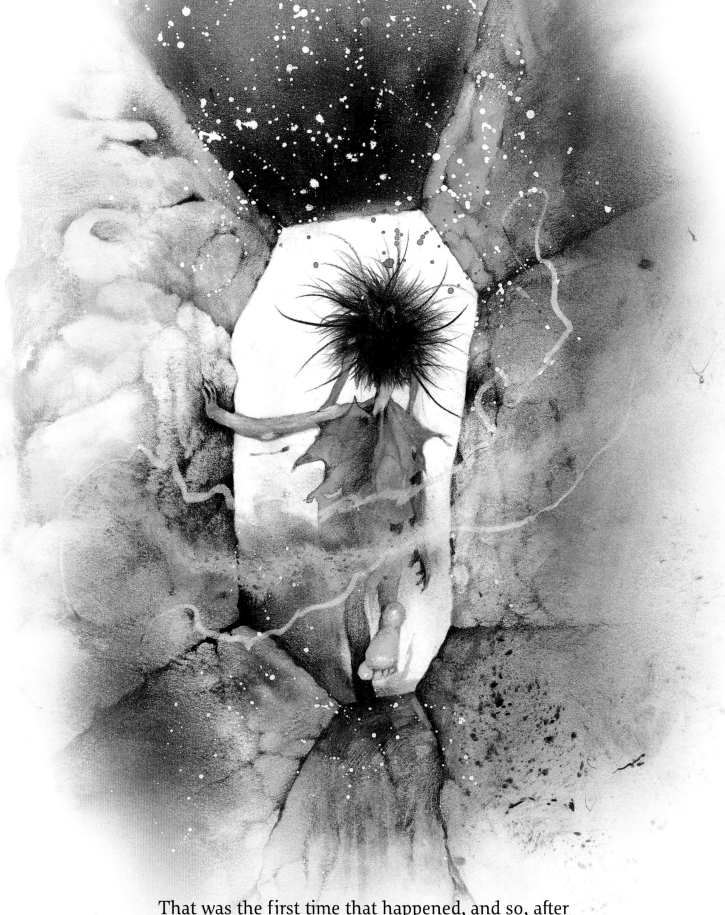

That was the first time that happened, and so, after
about four thousand three hundred and twenty-three years
and three months or so, the N𝕠ʙʙ𝕃e decided he'd had
enough: He didn't want to be alone anymore, and so he set
off to try to find some place he hadn't been yet, or maybe
see something there he hadn't seen yet . . . or something.

He really wasn't quite sure what he was going to
do, but he decided that maybe the glow way off in the
distance between Friday and Saturday might be a
place to start. He went past the place under the cliffs
where the fish sing, and turned left at the rock that
looks like you can climb it up to the moon
(though he hadn't done that yet),
and then he was farther
than he'd ever been from
the places he knew.

He was so far, in fact, that he kept seeing strange things. He saw some things that went high up into the air like mountains but were all shiny and square, and other things that were smaller with tilty things on their tops, and others with big flat gleaming things on their fronts. What the Nobble had found was what we call a city, and to him it was a very **unusual** place with very **unusual** things.

Like big, shiny, noisy box things, all different colors, that came zooming at him so fast he had to jump straight up in the air to get out of their way.

Then even bigger, roarier things, bigger than anything he'd ever seen, or at least anything that could move so fast, and he had to jump out of the way again, even higher this time.

Then he passed a big **fuzzy** thing that made such a
loud noise the N°BBLe thought his own long hair might
stand right up on end. And then another **fuzzy** thing
whose hair—when it saw the N°BBLe—did stand straight
up on end, and the noise it made,

$Yowhool$, was pretty scary.

And then, just as the NBBLe turned a corner, there
was this . . . other thing, with two long things, and two
other long things, and a round thing on top, and the
round thing had even longer hair than he had.

What it was of course was a girl, a little girl, and
when the little girl saw the N°BBLe she came running
toward him, saying, "Hey!" but the N°BBLe had seen
so many strange, scary things that he decided he'd better
run, so he did, as fast as he could, and though the girl
cried, "Wait!" the N°BBLe kept running, and though
she shouted, "Come back,"

he just kept running and running
until he couldn't run anymore.

"Oh, this could make you tired," thought the Nobble, standing there panting. "And this could even make you lonely, if you weren't already," he said to himself.

But still, he saw that way back behind him the little girl was still shouting to him, so finally the Nobble thought he'd better listen, except she was so far away he couldn't hear what she was saying. So, gathering his courage, the Nobble shouted back, "I can't hear you!"

And the little girl shouted even LOUDER, and finally he could hear her, but what she was saying was very strange.

What she was saying was, "Why don't you pick up the phone?"

"What's a phone?" thought the Nobble. Or he may have even said it aloud, because the little girl shouted,

"It's that thing in the glass box by the side of the road."

"What's a road?" said the Nobble, because mostly in his life he'd flown or swam or jumped over things, so he'd never had to walk or run on a road.

"It's that long flat thing you're standing on that goes off into the distance," the little girl's voice came again.

"Oh," said the Nobble, "and the phone is that glass thing next to the road?"

"No," the girl's voice shouted, "that's the *phone booth*. The phone is inside."

So the NOBBLE went over to the glass box, and there was a funny black thing in there.

"Is that black thing the phone?" asked the NOBBLE.

"YES," shouted the girl. "Pick up the phone."

So the NOBBLE picked the phone up. "This part looks like it goes by your ear," he yelled to the girl.

"YES," the girl's little shout came again. "Put it next to your ear."

"Like this?" said the NOBBLE.

"**YES!**" the girl said, but this time her voice was very loud, because it came over the phone. It was so loud, in fact, that the NOBBLE almost dropped the phone, but he kept listening.

"Whew," the little girl said in her regular voice. "I hope you can hear me all right. I'm tired of shouting."

"I can hear you just fine," the Nobble said. "But what do you want?"

"Well," said the little girl over the phone, "why don't you go over by the door?"

"What door?" said the Nobble. And then he said, "What's a door?" because he'd never actually seen a door until then.

"It's that big wooden thing right next to you there," said the girl.

"I see," said the Nobble, and he stood next to the door. "What am I supposed to do now?"

"Wait," said the girl, and just then THE DOOR MADE A NOISE.

"Boink!" the door said.

"Boink!"

The Nobble was so startled he almost fell down.

He called out to the girl on the phone. "It just made a noise. It said 'Boink!'"

"No," said the girl, "that's not 'Boink!' That's 'KNOCK!'"

"'Knock?'" said the Nobble.

"Yes," said the girl. "Listen again."

And sure enough, the noise was still coming out of the door, but this time instead of "Boink!" the Nobble heard "KNOCK!" Then he heard it again. "KNOCK, KNOCK, KNOCK."

"What do I do now?" asked the Nobble.

"Why you don't you answer the door?" said the girl.

Now let's not forget again that the Nobble had never seen a door, much less answered one, so he had no idea what you're supposed to say when you answer a door. So what he said was, "Where when?"

"KNOCK, KNOCK!" The noise came again.

"How so?" the Nobble said then. But there were just more knocks. "KNOCK, KNOCK!"

"Is why?" guessed the Nobble.

Then, "Why what?"

Then, "Hear who?"

"KNOCK, KNOCK!" came again, even louder.

And then, maybe by mistake, the Nobble said, really loud now, because he was getting tired of all this,

"WHO'S THERE?"

And through the door came of all things a voice.

"It's Me!" the voice said.

"Hurray," thought the Nobble, so he said,

"Who's There?" again.

And the voice in the door said back,

"It's Me!"

"What do I do now?" said the Nobble.
And the little girl said over the phone, "Why
don't you open the door?"

"How do you do that?" asked the Nobble.
(Don't forget that he'd never seen a door before.)

"You see that round thing on the door?" the
little girl said. "That's the knob. Pull on the knob."

Now the Nobble was not completely
comfortable about this, never having seen a knob
either, but he plucked up his courage, put his hand
on the knob, and pulled.

And the door started to open.

And then it was open. And someone, or something, was standing behind it.

"Yikes!" said the Nobble. "Somebody's there."

"Yikes!" said the someone who was there. "Somebody's here."

And the Nobble and the other person or whatever it was both hopped back a little, but then both of them stopped and looked at each other.

"You're a Nobble," said the Nobble.

"And you are, too—you're a Nobble, too," said the other Nobble.

"I thought I was the only person like me," said our Nobble.

"And I thought I was the only person like me," the other Nobble answered.

"This is wonderful," said our Nobble. "You have beautiful huge eyes and dangly ears and long hair and finger claws and a bunch of *very* nice toes. And you also look very friendly."

And the other Nobble said, "You look friendly, too. In fact, you look perfect. Would you like to be my friend?"

"I certainly would," said our Nobble. "It's a little sad out there in the twirls on top of the oak leaves and the swirls under the waves of the sea."

"I know," said the other Nobble. "Even in the curlicues inside flowers and the big boxes in shooting stars."

Just then the little girl ran up to the two N^{OBB}Le̊s. "You found each other," she said. "Isn't that splendid?"

"And you helped us," said our N^{OBB}Le. "I ran away, but you still helped me find my friend."

"I was trying to tell you," the little girl said, "that I'd seen someone who looked just like you, but you were so shy, you wouldn't wait."

"What's 'shy'?" asked the N^{OBB}Le.

"Well," said the little girl, "maybe shy is when you're lonely and you don't think anybody can help you."

"Well," said the N^{OBB}Le, "I'm glad you thought of a way to help me."

And the other Nobble said, "Us!"

And our Nobble said, "Yes, us."

And then he said to the other Nobble, "I know some places I'd love to show you."

"Oh," said the other Nobble, "and I have some things you might like, too. Shall we go find them?"

And our Nobble said, "Oh, yes, let's go . . . together."

Then he turned to the little girl and said, "Thank you, thank you so much for finding my friend. And . . . and . . . and . . ."

"Yes?" said the little girl.

"And . . . *here where* . . ." the Nobble said.

"What?" said the girl.

"And . . . *when whether,*" said the other Nobble. The little girl said, "What?" again.

"*If maybe?*" our Nobble said.

"*Therefore instead?*" said the other.

"What, what?" said the girl, who was a bit exasperated by now.

"We mean," said our N^oBB_Le, "that if we're going away, it seems as though we should say something, but neither of us has ever met anybody before, and so we've never had to leave anybody before, and so we don't know what you should say."

And the other N^oBB_Le said, "Do you say, '*How before*'? or '*Somewhere and then*'? or '*Over and ever*'?"

"Oh, I see," the little girl replied. "I know what you're trying to say. At times like this, when you're going away from someone you've met, you don't say, '*Here when*,' or '*If whether*.' What you say is, '*Goodbye*.' That's all, just '*Goodbye*.'"

"Hurray," said the N^oBB_Le. "I'll say that then: Goodbye, little girl."

"And I'll say it, too," said the other N^oBB_Le. "Goodbye, goodbye."

And then the two Nobbles turned to each other,
because there was a word that they guessed came along
with "Goodbye."

It was "Hello." So, "Hello, Nobble," our Nobble said.

"And hello, Nobble, to you,"
said the other Nobble.

Then, "Hello, hello," said both Nobbles at once. And they laughed, and ZOOMED OFF, both of them, up through the space of the highest note in your favorite song, then down through the bumpy part of that huge white cloud over your house; then they soared through the river that runs under the strings in a harp, and waved to the little girl, and laughed again, and crossed into the space between Wednesday and Thursday; and then the little girl couldn't see them anymore; all she could hear was their laughing,

and then they were gone . . .

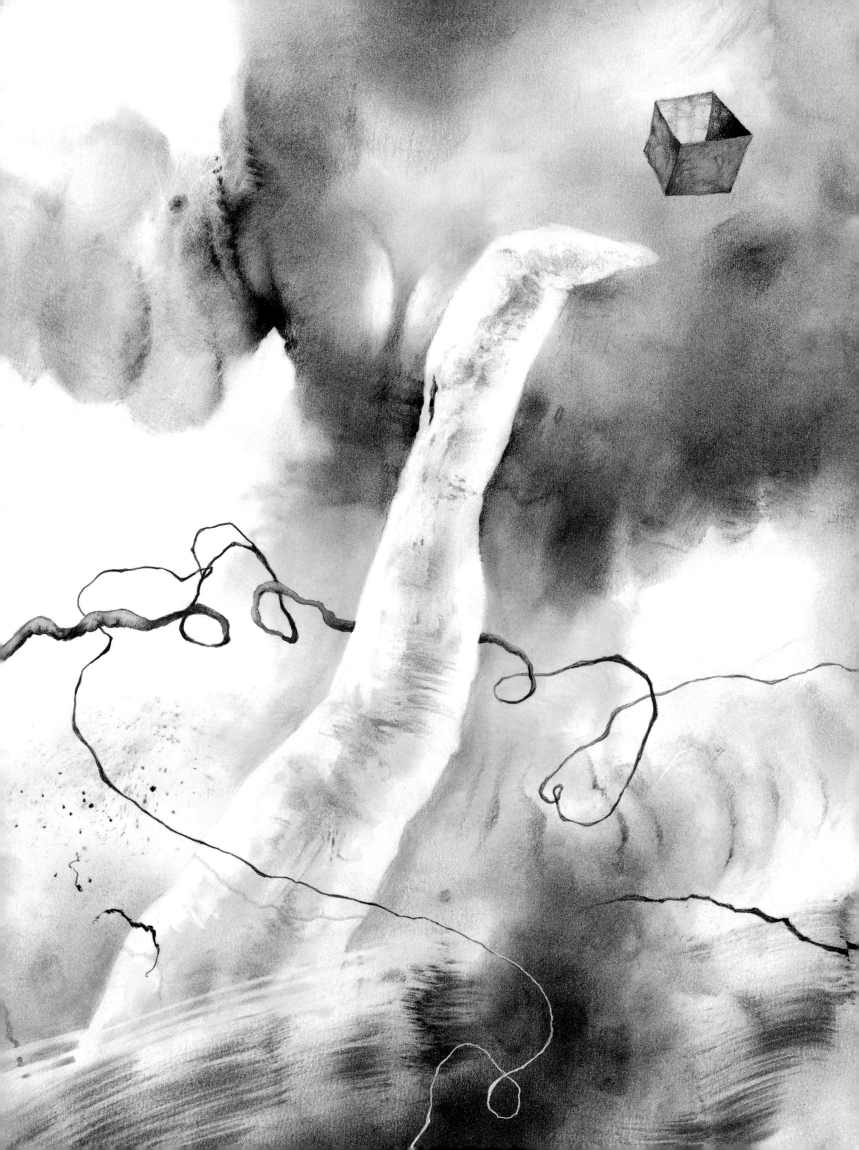

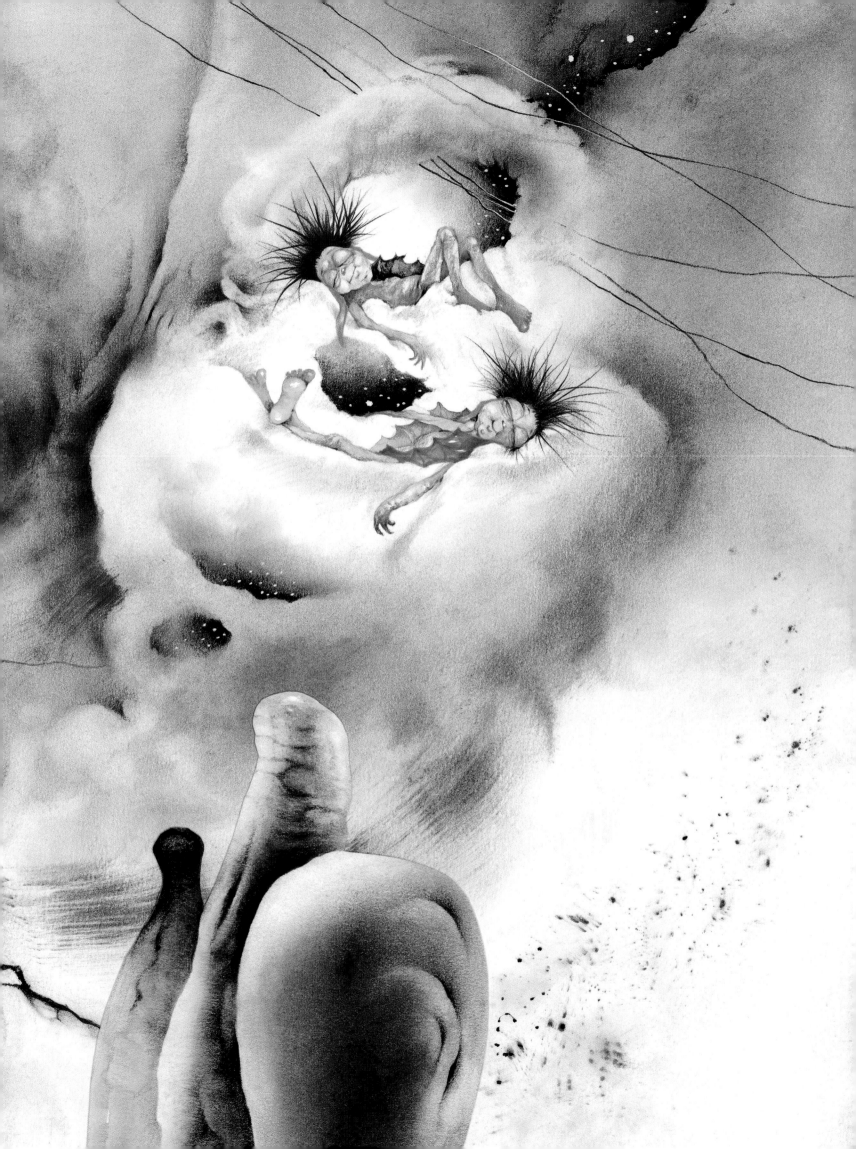

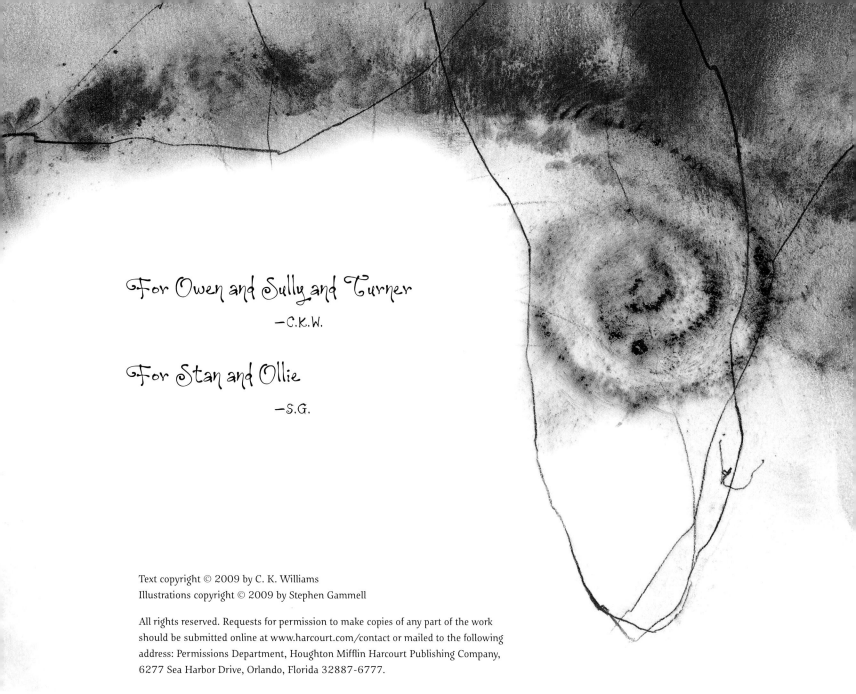

For Owen and Sully and Turner
—C.K.W.

For Stan and Ollie
—S.G.

Harcourt Children's Books is an imprint of Houghton Mifflin Harcourt Publishing Company.

www.hmhbooks.com

The handlettering was created by Stephen Gammell.
The text type was set in Sovereign.

Library of Congress Cataloging-in-Publication Data
Williams, C. K. (Charles Kenneth), 1936–
How the Nobble was finally found/C. K. Williams; illustrations by Stephen Gammell.
p. cm.
Summary: After many, many years of being alone, a Nobble finally finds a friend.
[1. Imaginary creatures—Fiction. 2. Friendship—Fiction.]
I. Gammell, Stephen, ill. II. Title.
PZ7.W655886Ho 2009
[E]—dc22   2008003285
ISBN 978-0-15-205460-1

First edition
H G F E D C B A

Printed in Singapore